For Akiko, with great fondness —F.W.

To Rebecca Lee, for listening and
encouraging through the seasons —J.U.K.

Text copyright © 1997 by Ferida Wolff
Illustrations copyright © 1997 by Joung Un Kim

For information about this and other Houghton Mifflin trade and
reference books and multimedia products, visit The Bookstore at
Houghton Mifflin on the World Wide Web at http://www.hmco.com/trade/.

The text of this book is set in 19.5 point Goudy.
The illustrations are acrylic, reproduced in full color.

Library of Congress Cataloging-in-Publication Data
Wolff, Ferida.
A year for Kiko / Ferida Wolff ; illustrated by Joung Un Kim.
p.   cm.
Summary: Each month of the year brings different activities for a young girl,
including catching snowflakes in January, planting a seed in May, and calling
to geese in September.
ISBN 0-395-77396-2
[1. Months — Fiction.]   I. Kim, Joung Un, ill.   II. Title.
PZ7.W82124Ye 1997   96-42537   CIP AC

Manufactured in the United States of America
WOZ 10 9 8 7 6 5 4 3 2 1

A Year for Kiko

Ferida Wolff ~ Illustrated by Joung Un Kim

Houghton Mifflin Company
Boston 1997

January snow is falling.
Kiko catches the snowflakes.
She slips in the snow.
The snowflakes catch Kiko.

February is cold and still.
Kiko's window is frosted white.
Kiko draws a smile with her finger.
The smile melts the ice.

Kiko's hat flies off!
March wind whips Kiko's hair.
Kiko puckers up and blows back.
"I am the wind," says Kiko.

April rain falls everywhere.
It waters the earth and Kiko too.
Now she must play inside.
Kiko cries raindrop tears.

Kiko plants a seed.

Maybe it will grow big.

Maybe it will become a pretty flower.

May is a month for maybes.

Kiko picks June strawberries.
One fat berry for the basket.
Many fat berries for Kiko.
Inside they become Kikoberries.

July fireflies glow in the night.
They blink their lights at Kiko.
Kiko chases them and laughs.
Her eyes are shining too.

August morning is hot.
Kiko wears her bathing suit.
She sits in her pool.
Now August feels cool.

Crickets chirp at Kiko.
Busy squirrels chatter.
Kiko calls to honking geese.
Together they sing a September song.

Red and gold leaves are falling.
Kiko holds a red leaf in one hand.
She holds a gold leaf in the other.
Kiko feels like an October tree.

Kiko looks for the moon.
The orange moon is hiding.
When Kiko hides, the moon finds her.
Kiko and the November moon are playing.

In December Kiko breathes out clouds.
She puts on her winter coat.
She wears her mittens and hat.
Kiko is ready for snow.